Wilfred's

Wilfred's Wolf

JENNY NIMMO

Illustrated by David Wynn Millward

RED FOX

A Red Fox Book

Published by Random House Children's Books
20 Vauxhall Bridge Road, London SW1V 2SA

A division of Random House UK Ltd
London Melbourne Sydney Auckland
Johannesburg and agencies throughout the world

Published by Red Fox 1994

1 3 5 7 9 10 8 6 4 2

Set in Plantin by SX Composing Ltd, Rayleigh, Essex
Printed and bound in Great Britain by
Cox & Wyman Ltd, Reading, Berkshire

RANDOM HOUSE UK Limited Reg. No. 954009

ISBN 0 09 930141 5

For chef Noel Cunningham

J.N. and D.M.

Wilfred's Wolf

One day a wolf crept out of a dark Arctic forest. He was fed up with gloomy skies, cold feet and loneliness. He wanted sunshine, excitement and a better diet.

Above all, he wanted a wife. There were none to be had in the forest behind him. Sometimes he thought he must be the only wolf left in the world.

The wolf's six senses all told him that the way to a better life lay in the south. So he set off down the long track that cut through icy mountains towards the sun.

The wolf travelled for three days and nights, only stopping to nibble the occasional frozen rodent. At the end of the third night he became very excited. He could smell something strange and wonderful and he could hear a mysterious sound. He began to run, and found himself in a noisy port. Beside the quay, men were loading fish on to a cargo ship, and the ship was sitting on a vast and glittering sea.

The wolf's adventurous spirit told him that the ship could carry him safely across the deep and dangerous water to happiness. He leapt aboard. None of the

sailors noticed him because it was a dark Arctic morning and they were all concentrating on their work. Nevertheless, the wolf decided that he had better hide until the ship had left port. He jumped down into a dark hold and found himself surrounded by fish. The hold was even colder than the gloomy forest and the smell was terrible, but the wolf did not dare to come out until the ship was bouncing over the sea. Even then he kept to the shadows and when he found a spare oilskin and sou'wester he slipped them on, just in case the sailors thought wolves were unlucky and threw him overboard.

Dressed in this way the wolf felt more confident. He began to strut about the deck, smart and carefree. He even peeped into the galley where the cook was frying the sailors' supper: steaming chips and sizzling sausages.

'Mmmmm!' The wolf smacked his lips. The smell coming from those big steel pans was utterly delicious.

'Hungry?' asked the cook, busily frying.

'You bet,' replied the eager wolf, forgetting to disguise his wolfish accent.

The cook knew every sailor on the ship and did

not recognize the wolf's deep voice. He looked up and
saw the long-nosed, hairy stranger.

'Hey!' he said. 'Who are you?'

The wolf did not know what to say. He slunk away
as the cook gave a piercing whistle and shouted, 'Stowaway!'

This frightened the wolf, who jumped back into the hold just as a gang of sailors came thundering across the deck. He squeezed himself between the crates while the sailors searched the cabins. They never bothered with the hold. 'If there's anyone down there, they'll freeze to death,' joked the captain.

Luckily the wolf had learnt to survive sub-zero temperatures, but he did find it very uncomfortable. For the rest of the voyage, the hungry wolf shivered and shook in the freezing hold. His big teeth chattered all night and this upset the rats who lived in the girders.

'Shut up,' they squealed. 'We can't relax,' and they threw fish-bone spears at him. Some of them even made bows and arrows and shot the poor wolf in the nose. He howled so loudly the sailors thought the ghost of a drowned man had come to haunt them, but they were far too scared to investigate.

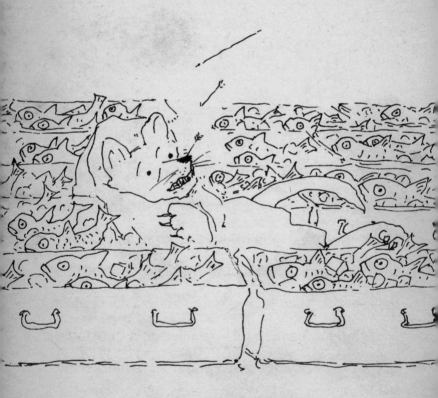

The tortured wolf removed the spears and arrows, closed his lips tight over his chattering teeth and tried to imagine that he was in a warm and friendly place.

At last the terrible journey was over. The wolf heard the bang and rattle, the hoot and clank of another busy port. He felt the roll and shudder of the ship docking and climbed out of his icy hiding place.

'Good riddance,' the rats called after him, but the sensible wolf kept his answering snarl to himself.

The sailors never noticed a hairy stowaway leap on to dry land and move swiftly through the crowd of dockers.

When the wolf saw a man loading fish into a blue van, he waited until the man had turned his back and then jumped inside. The man slammed the doors tight and the van sped away, down narrow streets, stopping, starting, hooting and growling. It was not at all like a

sea voyage. Just when the wolf thought he was going to

be car-sick, the van stopped. The driver came to open

the doors, and pulled out a box of fish. When he

walked away, the wolf followed. He crept across a cob-

bled courtyard and peeped through the door that the

19

van-driver had left open. At the end of a narrow passage, the wolf saw something thrilling and wonderful!

It was a room filled with golden pans, with steam
and smells, with tall white hats and magical utensils.
People shouted musical names, they sang and chattered and COOKED.

'I have reached it,' breathed the wolf. 'I have
reached the palace of my dreams!'

He waited until the man with the fish-box came
out and then he stole down the dark passage toward
the gleaming, humming kitchen.

Breathless with joy, the wolf walked into the very

heart of the dazzle and buzz, the sizzle and bustle of
the busiest kitchen in the world and, flinging wide his
arms, he sighed, 'Aaaaaaaaah.' His sou'wester fell off
and his open oilskin revealed his dreadfully hairy chest.

There was a pause in the cheerful bustle of the
busiest kitchen in the world. Expressions of horror and
disbelief passed across the flushed faces of the cooks

and assistants and a horrible truth dawned upon the poor Arctic wolf. He was not welcome!

He had barely taken in this disappointing news when a ripe banana hit him on the head. A boiled egg followed, then a tomato. And suddenly an avalanche of prickly pineapples, crockery, saucepans, ladles and knives came flying at the wolf. Men shouted in horrible bullying voices, women gave high-pitched unfriendly screams. It was all too much for the poor wolf.

Two large tears slid down his handsome grey nose. He realized how foolish he had been. He had travelled hundreds of miles all for nothing. He would never be loved or accepted by humans. He would never find a wife nor sit beside a cosy fire eating home-cooked food. He had better get going, back to the lonely frozen forest. He gave a moan of despair that could not be heard above the clamour of the kitchen weapons.

And then, suddenly, a voice roared, '**STOP!**'

A tall man dressed in clothes of unbelievable whiteness, strode up to the wolf and, placing a friendly hand upon his arm, said, 'Leave the poor fellow alone!'

'But, Wilfred,' cried a red-faced woman, 'he's a ...'

'I know he's a wolf,' said Wilfred sternly. 'So what? This is my kitchen and I'll choose the staff I want. If anyone dares to lay a finger on this good creature, I'll fire them. Got it? Now, back to your work immediately. Lord Salmon is waiting for his coq au vin.'

'Yes, Mr de Mornay,' came a chorus of suddenly meek voices.

'Allow me to introduce myself,' the tall man said to the wolf. 'I am Wilfred de Mornay, Head Chef of The Plush, which, as you probably know, is the biggest and best hotel in the world. I am very pleased that you have chosen to do your work-experience here.'

'I am just Wolf,' said the wolf, 'and I am very pleased, too.' He didn't know what work-experience meant, so he kept quiet about that part.

Wilfred invited him to observe how he made a pink sauce, and the wolf, while he watched, told Wilfred all about his lonely life in the icy forest and his terrible voyage in the freezing hold.

And then Wilfred told the wolf how he had always longed to meet a wolf. 'When I was a little boy my granny used to read to me,' said Wilfred. 'But she never read happy stories, they were always about boys who got into trouble, and they always had sad and terrible endings. The boys were beaten, locked up, starved, and eaten by lions. And if I moved an inch while she read, my horrible granny would hit me.'

The wolf was amazed to hear of all the nasty things that could happen to a small human. He began to think that the life of a cold, hungry wolf was better than being a beaten, starved and chewed-up child.

'One day,' Wilfred went on, 'my granny lost her book of horror stories. All she could find to read me was *The Tale of Red Riding Hood*. It was the most wonderful story I had ever heard for, instead of the child being eaten, it is the granny who gets her comeuppance. And guess who eats her?'

26

'Who?' the wolf asked breathlessly.

'A wolf, my dear fellow!'

The wolf was aghast. 'But I would never ...' he began.

'Of course you wouldn't,' said Wilfred. 'But some humans are just asking for trouble. Anyway, ever since that day I've longed to meet a wolf.'

By the end of the evening Wilfred and the wolf were best friends. Arm in arm, they walked into the moonlit yard of The Plush where Wilfred ushered the wolf into the back seat of his gleaming Rolls Royce. 'Put your feet up, dear chap,' he said, 'and travel in comfort for once.'

27

They rolled through streets of unimaginable brightness, past glittering windows and people of every shape, size and colour. The wolf was entranced. He never dreamt that there were even better things in store.

The Rolls Royce drew up outside a row of neat white houses. Each house had a small front lawn surrounded by pretty railings. The wolf followed Wilfred up a narrow path bordered with flowers and, as they approached the front door, the wolf heard a sound that made his heart leap in his chest. From inside the house there came a light, musical barking.

'Someone will be pleased to see you, Wolf,' said Wilfred with a wink, and he opened his front door.

The wolf beheld the most beautiful creature in the world. She was the answer to his dreams; a black-and-honey-coloured, long-lashed, silky-coated Alsatian.

'Wolf, meet Shirley,' said Wilfred. 'Shirley, this is Wolf.'

The radiant creature stepped forward and gave the wolf a welcoming kiss. The poor wolf almost collapsed with joy.

'He's a handsome fellow, isn't he?' said Wilfred.

Shirley fluttered her eyelashes. She was shy as well as beautiful. Side by side, the two animals followed

Wilfred into his kitchen, where he began to cook a meal for three. 'Shirley and I always have a midnight feast,' explained Wilfred. 'It's our favourite time of day.'

Shirley gazed at the wolf and murmured, 'Tonight it will be even better.'

After a delicious candlelit supper the wolf and Shirley fell asleep at the foot of Wilfred's enormous bed. But a little after dawn the wolf woke up and found that Wilfred had not come to bed.

There were sounds coming from the kitchen. The wolf tiptoed out to investigate. He found Wilfred, surrounded by pots and pans and bowls of steaming liquid. The table was littered with pies and pasties, puddings and petit-fours.

'Wow!' exclaimed the wolf. 'You work too hard, Wilfred.'

'I'm an insomniac, Wolf,' sighed Wilfred. 'I can't

sleep. I have to cook. It's the only thing that calms me down.'

'And do you eat all this food yourself?'

'Goodness me, no!' said Wilfred. 'Shirley has a little cart and she takes it round to all the local schools at lunchtime. Children love my cooking, and you'd be surprised how many forget their lunch boxes or hate school meals.'

'Would you teach me to cook?' asked the wolf. 'I have a sort of feeling about it. I cannot imagine anything more wonderful than to be a great chef.'

'I'd be delighted!' cried Wilfred. 'It will be so good to have someone to help me with my new recipes. Shirley isn't keen on that side of things. She's better at delivering.'

So the wolf had his first cookery lesson. He learned to make lemon meringue pie, and he did it so well that Wilfred realized immediately his new friend could be a brilliant chef.

Later that morning the wolf said goodbye to Shirley and set off with Wilfred for the smartest hotel in the world. In daylight The Plush looked even more magnificent. The wolf caught a glimpse of a great marble hall before Wilfred's Rolls turned into the courtyard at the back of the hotel.

When they heard that a wolf was going to work at The Plush every day, the other chefs, the waiters and kitchen staff, were naturally rather nervous. Wilfred had a hot temper, however, and he vowed that if anyone complained or told the manager, they would get the sack.

In a tall white hat and stiff bleached coat, the wolf did not look very different from the other chefs. And he soon proved to be an excellent cook.

He had very cool paws, which helped him to make exceptionally fine pastry.

He had a long, sensitive tongue, which he used to test all the subtle flavours in soups and sauces.

He had an acute sense of smell, which led him to choose the perfect herbs for casseroles and grills.

His eyesight was so good he could correctly measure the ingredients for a dessert without once using the scales.

Even his ears were useful, for he had such marvellous hearing he could tell by the tiniest crackle, sizzle or bubble exactly when a dish was ready.

But, most important of all, the wolf had FLAIR. It was his idea to add flower petals to his meals, so that

they not only tasted special, but looked exquisite.

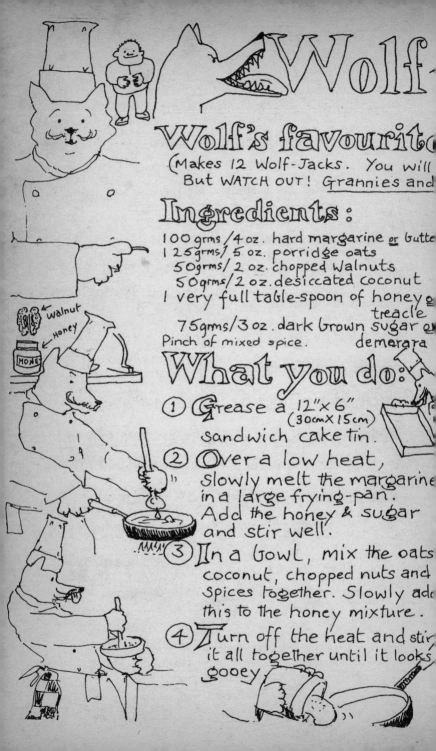

Wolf-

Wolf's favourite

(Makes 12 Wolf-Jacks. You will
But WATCH OUT! Grannies and

Ingredients:

100 grms / 4 oz. hard margarine or butter
125 grms / 5 oz. porridge oats
50 grms / 2 oz. chopped walnuts
50 grms / 2 oz. desiccated coconut
1 very full table-spoon of honey or
treacle
75 grms / 3 oz. dark brown sugar or
Pinch of mixed spice.   demerara

What you do:

① Grease a 12" x 6"
   (30cm x 15cm)
   sandwich cake tin.

② Over a low heat,
   slowly melt the margarine
   in a large frying-pan.
   Add the honey & sugar
   and stir well.

③ In a bowl, mix the oats
   coconut, chopped nuts and
   spices together. Slowly add
   this to the honey mixture.

④ Turn off the heat and stir
   it all together until it looks
   gooey.

Jacks

cookie recipe

(...ed a grown-up or a WOLF to help you.
...olves don't mix!)

5) Scrape the mixture into the cake tin and press down well with a spatula or clean paw

WATCH OUT THAT THE PAWS DON'T GET BURNT

6) Put on a low shelf in the oven on a very low heat (GAS MARK 2 or 300 F)

7) Bake for 50-60 minutes

8) Remove from oven with GLOVE

UNFAIR DIVISION →

9) Mark into 12 squares

FAIR DIVISION ↓

10) Lift out when cool.

Wolf it down

ZZZZ

24 WOLF-JACKS INDUCES SLEEP IN WOLVES

2-3 MAXIMUM DOSE FOR CHILDREN

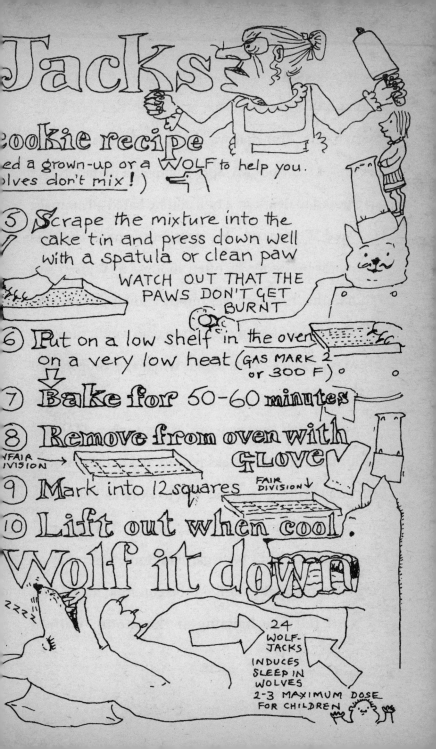

In a few days, everyone had learned to respect and admire him. Everyone, that is, except Mr Cyril Spite, the manager. But that was because no one had told him about the wolf. Mr Spite's father, a matador, had been gored to death by a bull and he hated all animals. He hated Wilfred, too. He thought the head chef was too big for his boots; he often shouted at Wilfred and told him that his sauce was lumpy and his greens were soft. Of course, this upset Wilfred who would turn and throw vegetables at Mr Spite while the soup boiled over.

So the wolf kept well out of sight when Mr Spite was around, and the weeks passed in a delightful way. Every day Wilfred took the wolf to work at The Plush. And every evening Shirley and the wolf would play together in Wilfred's back garden. Sometimes they all went for a midnight stroll on the common and if ever the wolf felt like howling at the moon, Wilfred

and Shirley would join in, so that their friend wouldn't feel silly.

One day the wolf noticed that Wilfred's behaviour was becoming very odd. He banged the saucepans more than was necessary, he scalded his fingers and broke jugs. Then, one steamy afternoon, he spilled fat on the floor. The under-chef slipped on the fat and went spinning across the kitchen with a bowl of cream. The cream flew into the face of a waiter,

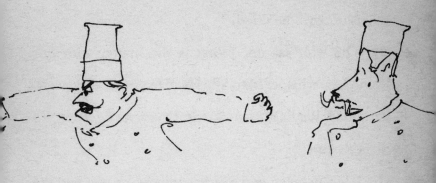

who gave an earsplitting yell. With a horrible growl, Wilfred threw a kitchen knife right across the room. It stuck in the wall only inches above the waiter's head.

'Mr de Mornay!' everyone cried. 'What is the matter?'

Wilfred wouldn't tell. Only Shirley knew her master's secret.

That night Wilfred was so tired he dropped into his big armchair and fell fast asleep. At his feet the wolf was lying, dreaming up new ways to cook a chicken, when Wilfred began to cry out in his sleep. 'Eclair! Eclair! Eclair!' he cried.

The wolf sat up. 'What is the matter with our friend?' he whispered to Shirley. 'He's been very peculiar today. Really rather violent. Everyone's getting fed up with him.'

'He's in love,' said Shirley gravely. 'A year ago the baker at The Plush was taken ill. Wilfred had to order all his cakes from the baker across the street. Eclair,

the baker's daughter, came over with a tray of meringues and Wilfred fell instantly in love with her. Every day, for a month, he asked Eclair to go out with him. He invited her to the movies, to the opera, to the theatre and to the ballet. He offered to take her to the seaside, to the country and to the forest. He said he would hire a boat, a private aeroplane or even a hot-air balloon. Eclair refused him, every time. She told Wilfred that all she wanted was to spend a week in Paris gazing at great works of art. Mr Spite will not give Wilfred a week off. He says he cannot find a replacement for him during the hectic summer season. Yet Wilfred feels that if he could only spend a week in Paris with Eclair, she would love him for ever, and probably marry him.'

While Shirley had been talking, the wolf had been thinking. A wonderful idea took shape in his head. He would take Wilfred's place. Wilfred had taught him so well no one could tell their cooking apart. He was sure that the staff of The Plush would support him. After all, they wanted Wilfred to be happy. All the knife-throwing and saucepan-banging made them nervous.

'Yes,' the wolf murmured, 'I shall take Wilfred's place.' He expected Shirley to laugh at such a suggestion but the beautiful Alsatian licked his face and said, 'Wolf, you are brilliant.'

Of course, they had to persuade Wilfred that the wolf could manage on his own while Wilfred was away. But Mr Pepper, the under-chef said, 'Wilfred, we'll all feel better if you have a break. We'll look after your wolf, don't worry. I will bring him to work in the morning and take him home at night. So, go and have your holiday.'

'You are all bricks,' said Wilfred, touched by their loyalty. He called on Eclair at the bakery that very afternoon. The wolf crept into the bakery behind

Wilfred. He watched the chef walk up to a beautiful girl and say, 'They have found a replacement for me, Eclair. I can take you to Paris for a week. Tell me you'll come.'

'Oh, Wilfred, I will, I will!' cried Eclair.

They held hands across a towering cake. Wilfred had never looked so happy. And then Eclair spied the wolf peeping round the door and asked, 'Who is that?' For a moment the wolf thought: I've ruined it all. And Wilfred thought: How can I tell Eclair I'm living with a wolf? He'll have to go or she will never marry me. Perhaps I can say that he's my grandfather? But, no, Eclair cannot be fooled. So risking all, he said, 'That is my best friend, Wolf!'

Wilfred and the wolf waited, their hearts beating furiously. Would Eclair scream and throw a bun at the wolf? Would she run away from Wilfred, for ever?

Eclair did none of these things. Instead she declared, 'I adore wolves. They are my favourite

animals. Why didn't you tell me about him, Wilfred?'
Then she took the wolf's paw and Wilfred's hand, and
they all danced round the baking table.

Next day Wilfred went to a travel agent. He booked two rooms at a famous hotel in Paris, and bought two airline tickets. That evening he packed his suitcase.

The wolf watched, nervously. He was excited, yet afraid. He didn't want to let Wilfred down.

Just before he left for the airport, Wilfred gave the wolf a friendly pat. 'Wolf, I can't tell you how much I appreciate what you have done for me,' he said. 'But please remember one thing. You must not let Mr Spite see you, even for a second. It would be disastrous.'

'I'll remember,' said the wolf.

On his first day as Head Chef of The Plush, the wolf walked into the centre of the busiest kitchen in the world and made a little speech. 'I would like to thank you all for allowing me to take Wilfred's place,' he said. 'When I was a cold and hungry wolf I learned to think of food as something precious and wonderful.

Now that I am in the land of plenty, I intend to cook thoughtfully, tenderly and magnificently. And I know that you will all help me to make the most delicious lunches and the most delightful dinners the customers have ever tasted. Thank you!' The wolf bowed to rapturous applause.

Unfortunately, Mr Spite popped in to see what all the fuss was about. The other chefs quickly gathered

round the wolf and said, 'It's Wilfred's birthday, Mr Spite. We're just having a little celebration.' So Mr Spite did not catch even a glimpse of the wolf's large ears, long nose and hairy paws.

The wolf was a tremendous success. News of the incredible and exciting food at The Plush spread quickly through the town and out into the countryside. People travelled great distances to taste the wolf's imaginative dishes. Of course, they never dreamed that their meals had been cooked by a wild animal. They praised the cooking and pressed generous tips upon the waiters.

Even Mr Spite was pleased. He went into the kitchen to congratulate the Head Chef. But the other chefs hid the wolf in a larder and told Mr Spite that Wilfred had been working so hard, he felt a little faint.

'Give him these,' said Mr Spite, handing them a bunch of flowers, a box of chocolates and a bag of money. 'Our regular customers have asked me to reward him for his excellent dishes.'

That night the wolf proudly showed his gifts to Shirley. 'The flowers and chocolates are for you, my darling,' said the wolf. 'But I would like to spend the money on a present for Wilfred.'

'Wolf, you are terrific,' said Shirley. 'I know that Wilfred wants a marble rolling pin. He threw his out of the window when Eclair turned down his invitation to the opera, and it smashed into a thousand pieces.'

'A marble rolling pin it shall be,' said the wolf. 'Marble, with silver handles.'

The following day he asked Mr Pepper to choose a special rolling pin for Wilfred. Mr Pepper was most impressed by the wolf's thoughtfulness. 'Wilfred will be very pleased,' he said.

The wolf was now so proud of his success he began to grow careless. He often forgot to put his hat on, and once he let his tail slip from under his apron. It knocked over a whole row of shellfish pyramids, which took hours to build up again. Sometimes the wolf would let out a little howl of satisfaction, surprising the waiters who would spill the wine and drop their trays. The wolf's friends begged him to be more careful, to remember that he was a chef now and not an animal. And the wolf tried, he really did. But, just a few hours before Wilfred and Eclair returned from Paris, the wolf, just for an instant, forgot himself completely and did something really foolish.

He had been too busy to stop for lunch and when, that evening, he found himself staring at a particularly juicy steak, he could not help himself. Without even picking up the plate, he bent down and sank his teeth into the thick, delicious meat. At that precise moment,

Mr Spite walked into the kitchen and came face to face with the wolf.

'A wolf!' screamed Mr Spite. 'That sneaky chef! That wretched Wilfred! He's such a bad cook he thought no one could tell the difference between his cooking and an animal's!'

This was too much for the wolf. He could not bear

to hear his friend insulted. Without thinking twice he lunged forward and bit off Mr Spite's bow-tie.

The manager's roar of fury echoed into the restaurant. 'Wolf! Wolf!' he yelled.

The customers leapt away from their tables and rushed outside calling, 'Wolf! Wolf! Call the police! Call the army!'

'Get it! Get it!' squealed Mr Spite running to the telephone.

For a moment the wolf was transfixed with terror.

Then he heard Mr Pepper's urgent whisper: 'Run, Wolf! Run!'

And the wolf ran.

He ran through the back door and out into the street. Cars hooted. People yelled. Sirens screamed. Bricks were thrown. Sticks and stones came flying.

Wherever he ran the wolf was met with a deadly and deafening human roar. He raced down dark alleys, through parks and gardens but he could not escape it.

At last he squeezed under a hedge and found himself in a moonlit cabbage patch. At the end of a path

stood a small garden shed. Battered and breathless, the wolf limped inside and lay on a pile of sacking.

'I shall have to go back to the lonely forest,' he moaned. 'I shall never see Wilfred and Shirley again.' And the wolf wept bitterly to think of the wonderful life he had lost.

At last the poor exhausted creature fell asleep, only to have nightmares about being chased through a city.

Meanwhile, Wilfred and Eclair had returned to hear the terrible news. They had become engaged to be married but their happiness was ruined by the wolf's disappearance and Shirley's tears. They could not bear to listen to the sirens and the megaphones. They put their hands over their ears and sat at the kitchen table, gazing at the wolf's last gift: a marble rolling pin with

silver handles, each one neatly inscribed, To Wilfred
Love Wolf.

And then Wilfred had an idea. 'It's just a chance,'
he said.

The wolf woke from his nightmares to hear a deep
voice saying, 'So that's where you are!' A powerful
light was beamed on him and a voice said, 'Come
quietly, lad! We don't want any more trouble, do we?'

So I won't even get back to the forest, thought the wolf. I shall have to spend the rest of my life in a human prison.

He padded sadly out of his hiding place and found himself looking at the bright buttons of a policeman's uniform.

But a surprisingly friendly hand was laid upon his neck. 'Don't fret, lad,' said the policeman. 'I'm P.C. Beagle, a mate of Wilfred's. I always take my wife to The Plush for her birthday. She's very fond of Wilfred's cooking, and yours, too, as it happens.'

The wolf could hardly believe his ears. The policeman's voice was so kind, so sympathetic.

'Wilfred's very upset,' went on P.C. Beagle. 'He called me as soon as he got home and heard about your little... mishap. And as for his dog, Shirley, she's in a dreadful state.'

The wolf moaned softly.

60

'Now, Wilfred has told me all about you,' went on
P.C. Beagle. 'He says that you are a well-behaved,
hard-working wolf and an excellent cook. I've also
interviewed the staff at The Plush and they all agree
with Wilfred.'

The wolf sighed.

'What's more,' said P.C. Beagle. 'I happen to have
a soft spot for wolves; my granny was a terror. So I feel

it's my duty to escort you home as quickly and quietly as possible. But keep this little meeting a secret, won't you? And, Wolf – don't let me down!'

The wolf glanced questioningly at the policeman who went on:.

'No biting grannies or hotel managers. No chasing pets or stealing meat. And try to keep the howling for special occasions like football matches and pop concerts, when everybody else is doing it too. Promise me, now!'

'I promise,' the wolf said solemnly. 'I want to be Shirley's husband and Wilfred's wolf for ever.'

By now everyone believed that the wolf had run off into the countryside. No one saw P.C. Beagle deliver him secretly to Wilfred's house. And no one saw the tears of joy, the hugging and kissing that went on behind Wilfred's front door, as Shirley, Eclair and the chef welcomed the wolf home.

They drew the curtains, set glowing candles on the table, and then they all sat down to a grand midnight feast.

Next day Cyril Spite was dismissed from The Plush. He had been hallucinating, said the staff, imagining a wolf in the kitchen biting off his bow-tie. 'The very idea,' scoffed Mr Pepper. 'His tie dropped in the soup.'

'We can't have that,' agreed the owner, Madame Ratatouille. 'Spreading wicked rumours. Mr Spite must go or The Plush will lose all its customers.'

Mr Spite left The Plush in disgrace and a very attractive manageress took his place. Her name was Elda Berry and everyone liked her, especially Wilfred, for she secretly confessed that she adored wolves.

So when the wolf came back to work in Wilfred's kitchen, Elda Berry pretended not to see his very

long nose or his furry ears. After all, he was an excellent cook and Elda Berry wanted to keep her customers happy.

And if any of the customers had been told that their food was cooked by a wolf, they would not have believed it. As a matter of fact, Wilfred and his wolf are still cooking at The Plush and probably will be for a long time to come.